Good, Brother

Peter Markus

Good, Brother

ISBN 0-9770723-5-5

Cover design and images: Derek White

Thanks to the following publications where some of these fictions also appeared: *3rd Bed, 5_Trope, Barnabe Mountain Review, Black Warrior Review, failbetter, Faultline, Flyway, LitRag, Massachusetts Review, Metro Times Literary Quarterly, New Orleans Review, New Sudden Fiction, Northwest Review, Quarterly West, Sudden Stories, Third Coast,* and in a limited edition book published by AWOL Press.

Published by Calamari Press, NY, NY

www.calamaripress.com

Contents

In the beginning was the word,

and the word was mud.

John 1:1

Good, Brother

We used to take the fish we'd catch out of this dirty river that runs through this dirty river town and we used to cut off those still-glistening-with-silver-scaled heads and we used to nail them, those heads, into the backyard telephone pole out back behind our yard. We'd hammer nails into those fishes' cold-water-eyed heads and make for ourselves what my brother and me used to call our backyard fishing pole. We did not stop fishing for and catching and nailing those fishes' heads into wood until the day our father came home from work and told us we were leaving. When our father told us we were leaving, he meant it, we were leaving for good: this dirty river, this dirty town. We did not want to leave, my brother and me. We did not want to leave behind the town or the river or the fish-headed telephone pole that the two of us brothers turned into a back-of-the-yard fishing pole out back behind the backyard shed where our father kept his hammers and his saws and his cigar boxes full of rusty, bent-back nails and his nuts and bolts and screws and those bottles of his half-filled up with whiskey.

At night, from our bedroom's window, my brother and me could look outside and see those fishes' marbly-looking eyes looking back all walleyed out from the sides of their chopped-off heads. The biggest of the big-lipped fish looked like they might leap out and bite the hand left dangling over the side of a boat. Each of the fish heads, us brothers, we gave each one a name. In the end there were exactly a hundred-and-fifty fish heads named, each with its own name. Not one was called Jimmy or John.

Jimmy and John were my brother's and my real names. But we called each other Brother.

Our father called us brothers Son. When our father hollered out, Son, the both of us brothers would turn back our boy heads. We both knew, we were crossing this river together.

Our mother called us brothers her dirty little boys. Us brothers were made, our mother liked to say, in the muddy image of our father. We did not like it much when our mother made us wash the mud from off the bottoms of our muddy boots.

We liked mud and those dirty river smells that smelled of fishing and worms. We did not like it when our mother made us wash our hands to rid ourselves of those fishy river smells. We liked the way the fishes' silver fish scales stuck to and glittered sparkly in our hands. At night, we liked to hold our hands up to the moonlight shining into our bedroom window. It looked like our hands had been dipped in stars.

But our mother and our father both were sick and tired of living in a town with a dirty river running through it and with river winds that always smelled of fish. Our mother said she wanted to go somewhere, *anywhere* is the word she used, so long as anywhere was west of here. West where? was what our father wanted to know. And what our mother said to this was, West of all this muddy water. Somewhere, our mother said, where there's not so much mud and rusted steel. There's a bigger sky, our mother wanted us brothers to know. There's a sky, our mother told us. There's a sky not stunted by smokestacks and smoke.

Us brothers couldn't picture a sky bigger than the sky outside our backyard. We didn't want to imagine a town without a dirty river running through it where we could run down to it to fish. We did not want to run or be moved away from all this smoke and water and mud.

We didn't know what we were going to do, or how we were going to stay, until we looked outside and saw our fish. The fish heads were looking back at us, open-eyed, open-mouthed, and it was like they were singing to us brothers. That night, us brothers, we climbed outside through our bedroom's window. Only the moon and stars were watching us as we walked out back to our father's tool shed and dug out his hammers and a box full of rusty, bent-back nails. We each of us brothers grabbed a handful of nails and a hammer into each of our hands and walked over to our fish-headed telephone pole. Brother, I said to Brother, you can go first.

Give me your hand, I told him. Hold your hand up against this wood.

Brother did like I told.

We were brothers. We were each other's voice inside our own heads.

This might sting, I warned. And then I raised back that hammer. I drove that rusty nail right through Brother's hand.

Brother didn't even wince, or flinch with his body, or make with his boy mouth the sound of a brother crying out.

Good, Brother, I said.

I was hammering in another nail into Brother's other hand when our father stepped out into the yard.

Son, our father called out.

Us, our father's sons, we turned back our heads toward the sound of our father.

We waited to hear what it was that our father was going to say to us brothers next.

It was a long few seconds.

The sky above the river where the steel mill stood like some sort of a shipwreck, it was dark and quiet. Somewhere, I was sure, the sun was shining.

You boys remember to clean up before you come back in, our father said.

Our father turned back his back.

Us brothers turned back to face back each other.

I raised back the hammer.

I lined up that rusted nail.

What We Do with the Fish After We Gut the Fish

We eat the fish. Our mother fries up the fish in a cast-iron skillet that spits up buttery fish fried grease every time she drops a breadcrumb-battered fish fillet into the pan. We sit at the kitchen table in front of our empty plates and listen to the pop and pizz and sizzle of the frying-up fish. Just yesterday these fish were swimming in the muddy waters of our muddy river and now they are gutted and headless and chopped in half and about to be swallowed into our open mouths, our empty bellies. Our father is back outside, back in the shed, sharpening up his knives. When all the fish have been fried up hard to a crisp-shucked golden brown, our mother will tell us brothers to call in our father to come inside to eat the fish. Fish on, we tell our father. Come and get them while they're good and hot. Our father comes when us brothers call. Us brothers stand back and watch as our father tracks mud into our mother's kitchen. Our mother tells our father look what you've done. Our father looks down at his muddy boots and utters the word mud. Our mother throws up her hands and then she throws the frying pan of fried-up fish at our father. We watch our dirty river fish skid across the kitchen's floor. Our father tells our mother that he and us sons fished for and caught and cleaned out the guts out of those fish. Our mother tells our father that he knows what he can do with those fish. Then she tells us how she hates fish and fish smells, how she hates this dirty, fishy river, how much she hates this fishy, smelly town. Then leave, our father says to this. Our mother says maybe she will. They both turn and walk away then, our father back outside, our mother into hers and our father's bedroom. Us brothers, we are left with the fish, are left to clean up the mess. We drop down onto our hands and knees, onto the floor, and begin to eat.

Our Father's Shed, Where Our Father Keeps his Tools, the Rusty Buckets & Muddy Shovels, the Nuts & Bolts & Screws, Bottles Half-Filled with Whiskey

Our father's backyard shed, where our father keeps his tools, his rusty buckets and muddy shovels, the nuts and bolts and nails and screws, the bottles half-filled with whiskey: this shed, it's not made out of mud: it's made out of wood, what our father likes to call lumber, and us brothers, our father's sons, we like it the way that word lumber sounds when it lumbers out of his, out of our father's, fish-lipped mouth. On our father's tongue, this word, lumber, when it comes lumbering out, it sounds even heavier than lumber itself.

Hand me up that lumber, our father says to us. He says, Son, hand me up my hammer. Us brothers, we do what our father says. We take our father's hammer into our boy hands and we hand our father his hammer. Then we step back and watch our father cock back with his hammering hand and then we watch him hammer in his other hand, his nail holding hand, into wood. When that rusted, bent-back nail goes through his hand and into the lumber that is behind it, our father doesn't even flinch, or wince, or make with his mouth the sound of a father crying out. What our father does do with his mouth is he says to us brothers who are doing this watching, This wood is good wood. This is a good piece of lumber, he says, and he sucks in on the second rusted nail pinched in the corner of his mouth. Now it's your turn, he turns, and says this to us brothers, and he spits out this bent-back nail. Us brothers, we look across at each other, we glance down at this nail that is here on the dirt between us, we gaze up to see our father's hammered-in hand, his fingers flaring out like the fin of some still-live fish when we stick in the knife to gut it. What we see, here in our father's

.

hammered-in hand, are rivers and rivers rivering out from the head of this rusted, bent-back nail. Us brothers, we both of us know, we are crossing this river together. We give each other this look. There is this look that us brothers sometimes like to look at each other with. It is the kind of a look that actually hurts the face of the brother who is doing the looking. Imagine if you would that look. We keep looking with this look. Then, us brothers, we reach up and put our hands on top of our father's, and we hold him here in this place.

Our Father Who Walks on Water Comes Home with Two Buckets of Fish

This is our father we are watching. We watch our father walk on water. He is walking across it: our father is crossing this dirty river that runs through this dirty river town: our father, he is coming back now from the river's other side. We see that he has, hanging from each one of his muddy hands, a muddy bucket hanging. When it is us, his sons, that he sees are the ones doing the watching, our father walks up to face us. He sets down those muddy buckets down onto the ground. We look down at those buckets. When we look down inside of these buckets, we see that they are both filled up to the rusted brim with fish. Supper, our father says to this. Let's go home and fry up these fish. Us brothers, we do what our father says. We shadow our father home, us mudding through the mud, us brothers walking in the mud-left tracks of our father's muddy boots. When we get home, we watch our father walk into the kitchen without first taking off his boots. Us brothers, we do like our father. We walk inside, into the kitchen, with our boots still on our feet. The floor, with mud muddied all across it, it has never looked so shiny. Mother, our father calls out. We listen to him call out her name. Us brothers, we don't say anything about our mother. We go and fetch us a frying pan out of the cupboard and we put it on top of the stove. Our father sees us brothers and gets himself a knife to gut the fish with. Maybe what our father is figuring is that our mother is out shopping. Our father takes the fish up and out of the buckets and he goes at the fish with this knife: he cuts off first the fish's head, the tail next, then he sticks the rusted blade up inside. We watch our father claw two fingers in and slide them up inside this fish. What is inside the fish comes slushing out onto the kitchen's floor. When our father is done gutting the fish, us brothers, we fry the fish up hard in sputtering hot butter, what our father likes to call lard. It's good to be back home, boys, our father says. We sit down at the table to eat. Our father, he calls out for our mother to come eat with us boys. When he gets no answer, only the rivery echo of a motherless house, our father keeps on eating. We keep on eating. Us brothers, we do not say a thing about our mother. After we are done doing this eating, it is us brothers who do the cleaning up. We take what is left off of our dirty dishes and we scrape what's left into the trash. The dirty dishes, slick with fish and butter, we pile these up into the kitchen's sink. The parts of the fish that we do not eat—the guts, the heads, the skins, the bones—these we take outside, out to the back of our backyard. The guts, the tails, the skins of the fish, these us brothers bury, in holes that we, us brothers, dig. The fishes' heads, with the marbly-looking eyes still staring out of them, we hammer these heads into the backyard telephone pole out back in the back of our yard. It's the sound of us brothers doing this hammering that brings our father back outside. When our father asks us brothers, where is your mother, one of us brothers whispers, *fish*, and the other one of us mutters that other word, *moon*. To this, these two words, words that are the world to us brothers, our father nods his head, up then down, then he heads back down towards the river. And without a word or a wave goodbye to us brothers, we watch our father walk back across the river, back to the river's other side, walking and walking and walking on, until he is nothing but the sound that the river sometimes makes when a stone is skipped across it.

Muddy Truck, Rusty River

We hop up into what used to be our father's rusted, muddy truck, our faces barely sticking up above the mud-dusty steering wheel, our noses nosing up beyond the even dustier dash, where our dirty boy hands have left their fingers' dirty prints in the filmy dirt, and the two of us brothers drive, down to the muddy river, down to the water where so much of our life takes place, us, going slow now, taking the long way through this dirty river town, this, to give what's no longer a piece of our father, our father's rust-pitted pickup truck, a last showing, a final hurrah, this, all done in the beautiful rain, this, in the lateness of night, the town's people put up in their beds, or hunched over in bars, or parked in front of their TVs, the streets left to their loneliness, the town's lone traffic-light blinking yellow from all four sides—us, brothers, look at us, trucking our way down the river line, the river and the river winds and those rivery smells of fish and worms always at our river sides, us, slowing down now, after a while, and us brothers cutting the wheel and pointing it straight ahead into the river's face, us in our father's truck gassing it down to where the river's road runs itself out into a dead-end, do-not-go-any-further point in this story, a rusted metal guardrail telling us brothers to turn this truck back, turn ourselves back around, that this, the beginning of this dirty river, this is the end of our dirty river road. But this, no, this: this is not what us brothers want you to see. What we want you to remember is, what we want to leave you with is, it is not the sign that says on it, No Motor Vehicles Allowed Beyond This Point. What us brothers want to point out, what we want you to pay attention to, is us brothers paying all of this no mind. What we want you to see is us brothers going on, us pushing past, us brothers steering around, going beyond this point, us brothers riding up onto the mud and the grass, us brothers bumping forward, and onward, onto where the grass is mostly just rocks and mud and dirt, down to where the river's muddy water has risen up and over and is flowing up past its muddy river bank: look, that is, to the river, to where river is at its edgy beginning, here where water and dirt mix to make mud. Keep looking, too, because us brothers, we do not stop there. We keep mudding on, our wheels in the mud sometimes spinning, the spinning rubber kicking up mud, a brother's muddy boot punching itself down on top of the gas pedal, flooring it down to the floor until there's only river beneath us brothers, it's just the river that is holding up this mud-rusty truck: this dirty river, it is floating this thing of steel up, our father's truck, it is no longer our father's, this rusty truck, it is held now in the muddy hands of the river. It's the river that is lifting us brothers up, just briefly now, before we, us brothers, and it, our father's truck, we begin our sinking down, the river creeping inside with us brothers, past our muddy-booted feet and then up to our always-dropping-down-in-the-mud knees, the river's dirty water rising up and up and up, faster now, until us brothers are forced to push ourselves up, us brothers, we raise ourselves up, and out, the pickup's open windows, and what us brothers want you to notice now is not us brothers kicking our legs to swim away, our arms wheeling against the water, not us brothers paddling back to where the river turns back to mud. What we'd like your eyes to gaze upon is this truck, this hunk of rusted metal that our father might've one day made, back in the day when he was making it, it is gone to rust and mud and it is going under now: the hood, with the engine underneath it, the heavy end going down first. Then watch the back bed of this pickup, empty, the tailgate, taillights, silver bumper: these are the last of this truck to go. So see it go: watch it go away, watch it like the way, in a different time, us brothers might have stood back and watched our mother and father drive away from us brothers, down some muddy back-road, away from this dirty river town of ours, off on a second honeymoon, maybe (it could have, it should have been), with us brothers left to be just with ourselves, us brothers standing off to the side of the road, or else maybe in the middle of it, watching and waving with our hands held in the air, us brothers staying there, inside that moment, until the red brakelights flashed on, then back off, before turning that corner to head out to the highway outside of town. But no, our father and mother are not in that driving-away car. Our father walked out of the picture a good while ago, and our mother, she is now a bed in a bedroom with a door that does not like to open up. So when our father's truck sinks out of our sight, and the river goes back to being a dirty river, not a river with a truck sinking down in it, us brothers, we get this feeling inside of us that is like something rising up on the insides of our spines. We are lighter now, us brothers: a truck has been lifted up off of us. And us brothers, arm in arm, see this, believe in this, this is us brothers believing in ourselves: this is us brothers, are you watching us now, this is how the both of us brothers learned how to fly.

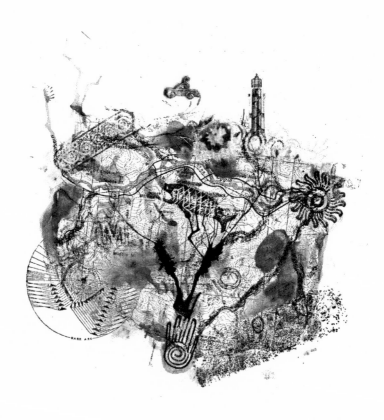

The Moon is a Lighthouse

Our house is an island floating in a river of mud and rust and light. See the two of us brothers swimming in a pool of the sky's spilt milkiness. Picture us brothers: fish fins turned to boy fingers, boy lips in the place of fish gills, gasping in to breathe in the thick, smoky, unwatered air—brothers playing kissy face with the muddy sky. We throw our bodies down, onto the ground, and find staring back up at us brothers the beginning of, the mud at the bottom of the world, of what'll be made to be Girl. Look here, us brothers say, to each other. We see eyes, and a nose, and a mouth. We see lips. Kiss me, we say, to the mud. Us brothers, we are bellies down in the mud, poking, prodding the muddy ground with our fingers. We plunge our hands in up past our wrists, mud up to our elbows, until we are kneeling on our elbows and knees with mud up to our navels, mud up to our necks. This is when Girl stands up in the mud, rises up from the mud, girl ankles and calves and knees, girl legs that seem to reach up into the moonless sky. Girl could be holding in her girl hands a torch made out of fire, a light to light the way for ships looking for harbor. Us brothers, we climb up to the top of Girl, up a ladder made out of mud and rust and light, until we reach a crown stitched from the lint of clouds. Down below us, nipping at our heels, the sky is a river flowing over with mud and singing fish. Each star in the night is a ship-lit buoy, and the moon is a lighthouse with an old man living inside it.

The Moon is a Fish

Once, when one of the fish that us brothers caught, a fish that we lured and hooked and reeled in and up onto our river's muddy banks, this fish, it was so beautiful, it was such a lovely fish, its fish eye moons, its fish scales glowing stars, that us brothers could not bring ourselves to kill and to cut off this fish's head. We'd never had any trouble cutting off the heads of any fish before we did with this beautiful fish. Beauty, this fish, this thing of beauty, it was messing with us brothers' muddy heads, it was a rusty nail running its way through our muddy brother hearts.

So we decided to bring this fish home with us, and there we ran a tub full of cold water in the bathroom's claw-footed tub, and with our boy hands curled tenderly around the fish's beautiful white belly, we lowered this fish into this water. Here in the tub, this fish kissed and bumped its fish nose up against these walls. When this fish swam twice around the tub, it stopped with its swimming and looked up at us brothers, us who were looking down at it, watching this fish tread water, marveling at this fish with our eyes and our hands and our boy mouths hanging quietly open, the way we do when we look up to see the moon.

Mud, this fish said, this word, mud, the sound of this word, mud, bubbling up at us brothers. Muddy water, this fish said next, its fish mouth a lilted flower, its fish lips lifting up to blow us brothers a final kiss goodbye.

Brother looked over at me then and I looked over at Brother. Us brothers, we both knew, in our muddy hearts, our muddy heads, what it was that we had to do.

The river.

We ran ourselves down to the river, with a metal bucket, to fetch our fish brother some mud, some muddy water. We dug in with our boy hands into the mud. This bucket, us brothers, we filled it up with mud. Then we ran ourselves back to our house and we dumped the mud from this bucket into the tub. The water turned a sudden and beautiful muddy brown. The fish looked up at us brothers, up from all this mud, up, and up, through the muddy water. A fish, at this moment, never looked more beautiful. Its eyes were unnamed planets. Each scale on this fish's slender fish body was a burning kiss left by a falling star. Us brothers, we bent down the both of us onto our knees and reached in to touch the fish. You, come on, reach in with us brothers and touch this fish. This fish is a thing you can touch only once. Touch it twice and its beauty will banish you with beauty. Each of us brothers, after a while, we picked up this fish. We held it up against our chests. Us brothers, like this, we looked at each other. There was this look that us brothers liked to sometimes look at each other with. It was the kind of a look that actually hurt the eyes of the brother who was doing the looking. Imagine that look. After we were done doing this looking, without saying a word, us brothers, the both of us, we ran back down to the river. We kissed this fish goodbye. We threw this fish back, into the river, and the river, this muddy river, this beautiful river, it kissed us brothers back.

Boy

We knew this other boy in town who was brother to nobody—an only child with only a mother and a father and no brother to call his own. So we took him in as brother. We did not call him brother though. We called him Boy. Boy was littler than us brothers. Boy was born years—no, centuries— after we were born. We were down by the river with our fishing man father the day that this boy was born into this world. This boy, this brother, we were told, was born with teeth and a full head of hair. What he was not born with, we discovered, was a tongue. This boy's mouth was a hole in his face he fed food into. Once in a while, we might hear some mouthy sounds come grunting out. But for the most part, Boy was silent. Some of the time we did not even know he was near us brothers, standing close by, his feet—flopping inside his father's boots—buried knee deep in the river's mud. At times, Boy was more dog than he was a boy. Boy was a dog who always came whenever we called, to do whatever we told. Us brothers taught Boy more than a few tricks. We taught Boy how to walk on water. It's true that Boy drowned the first time he walked out. Boy floated face down down the river. But then he walked upriver back. Back to us brothers. Good dog, we told Boy. We scratched Boy's back. We pulled a bone out from Boy's hand and tossed it to the river. Boy, we told Boy. Go fish. Boy took to that muddy river water like he was part dog, part fish. Then Boy swam back to the river's muddied bank and flopped down on the shore. Yes, just like a fish. This boy here is a keeper, Brother said. If you say so, I said to Brother. And then we chopped off this boy's head.

We Make Mud

We make Girl.

We make Girl down by the river out of the river's mud. Here, where river water meets earth to make mud we make Girl. We start at the bottom and make our way up. Girl's knees are especially muddy. They make us want to remain forever kneeling. Us brothers, we can barely stand to look Girl straight in the eye. She is that muddy. Her girl eyes and her girl hair and her girl skin too, all the color of mud.

We love mud.

Mud, us brothers, we can never get enough of mud.

Girl is pure mud. Even her girl heart is made out of mud. Her mud heart drums inside her mud chest. Like a drum made out of mud. If you close your eyes, you can see it, Girl's heart, see it? It is shaped like a star. If your cup your hand up around your ear, to make it into a shell, you can hear it, Girl's mud heart: it is a drum drumming to us brothers to come hear. Make mud is what Girl's heart tells us. Make more mud.

When it rains, Girl calls out to us to come save her. When it rains, us brothers, we bring Girl inside, into our bedroom. We tuck Girl into bed and kneel by her girl side.

If it looks as if we are saying our prayers, look again. We are watching Girl sleep.

In the morning, us brothers, we each take turns kissing Girl on her girl lips, to breathe her back into this other life.

Girl is our sister.

Our mother and our father both think we are just two brothers. They think we are sisterless.

They are wrong.

Girl is all ours.

We made her.

Girl began as mud.

Girl began as mud but became a girl when we gave her her name. We named her Girl because that's what she looked like: girl. Girl, we said. And the name stuck like a stick stuck in the mud.

We took a stick and spelled Girl's name in the mud down by the edge of the river.

G-I-R-L.

Girl looked good in mud.

Girl's mud body shined like something made brand new in the moonlight.

Girl was made naked.

Brother was the brother of us who pointed this out.

Yeah, I said. So?

Brother said, She needs some clothes.

Who says? I said.

Maybe she's cold, Brother said.

Are you cold? I asked Girl.

Girl didn't say anything.

Brother left though and when he came back he was holding in his arms a bag full of girl clothes.

I asked him where he found those.

Inside our mother's closet, Brother said.

I looked at Brother.

There was this look that us brothers had between us.

It was a look that actually hurt the eyes of the brother who was doing the looking.

Imagine that look.

Where else was I supposed to look?

I didn't know.

So I took back the look.

We got Girl dressed.

We pulled our mother's skin over the head of Girl.

Even so, Girl was still beautiful.

Girl's body shined, like wet mud it was shining, from beneath our mother's cottony clothes.

Girl

We were all of us naked. Us brothers, the both of us brothers, we were naked beneath our clothes. We were naked but I knew neither one of us would say so. So I went ahead and said what I always said. What I said was, Hey Girl. I liked that word G-I-R-L. I liked to call Girl, Girl. Girl, I said. Girl, I wish I knew what to do with my dirty boy hands. My hands, I knew, were hands that smelled of fish and wormy fish dirt. Hold up your hands, Girl said. Like this. Girl held up her hands, fingered tips up, her narrow girl palms facing my squared off boy face. I held up my hands. I might have been saying, I give up. Now what? was what I said. Girl leaned her body in close enough to touch. She lowered her hands. Girl's hands fell down to cup and huddle round her curved-by-the-river hips. Close your eyes, Girl said. Then: Don't open them until I tell you. There was this light hovering just outside the edges of darkness hiding out behind the lids of my eyes. I tried but I could not make out Girl's face hiding anywhere nearby. It was like I was being held underwater. Good, Girl said. I could hear the river whispering in my ears. I knew right then I was in that place where I had always wanted to be. It was like walking on water. Or like talking to the face of Girl. Okay, Girl said. Now open your eyes. I could feel Girl's heart hammering away inside her chest. I could see it beating, too. Girl's heart wasn't shaped like a heart. It was shaped like girl: like the word, girl. Like the word, girl, scrawled in mud. Like the way that word, girl, was meant to be spelled: with twelve r's, thirteen u's, and twenty thousand l's at the end of girl, stretching across the earth.

Star Fish

Our knuckles, Girl said, are rivers. Our knuckles, Girl said, are rivers that run deep. See, Girl was always showing us brothers how to see. Look, Girl added, your hands. She took hold of our dirty boy hands and held them up against her chest. Your hands are star fish washed up from an ancient sea.

> See the sun, Girl said.
> It is fire.
> And the moon? Girl pointed up.
> We nodded without looking up.
> The moon, Girl said. It is an eye.

Whose eye?

This, Brother wanted to know.

Girl gazed down her nose at both of us brothers. There was this light that shined out.

The moon is a light above the river.

It is a lighthouse.

Its light is a rope the moon throws down to save the river.

It is my eye, Girl said.

Girl reached up to pluck the moon from the sky.

Girl made it look so easy.

The moon is a skinned apple, Girl said.

Girl ate the moon.

The next night a new moon grew back.

The Moon is a Mirror

Sometimes, Girl slips her hands in through our bedroom's window and pets my brother's and my's peach fuzz cheeks. When this happens, we try not to wake. If we wake, we make like we are still sleeping. Girl holds our sleepy heads in the palms of her mud cracked hands and rocks us to keep us sleeping. Sometimes, Girl sings. Some nights, Girl lifts us up and holds us to her chest, there where the treasure of her heartbeat is buried beneath her skin. There is a freckle there, a beauty mark, above Girl's heart. It is shaped like an X. Dig here is what her heart tells us. Us brothers, we always listen. In the morning, us brothers awake with a mission. We get our father's shovels and head on down to the river, to where Girl whispered to us that she would be waiting. She is. So we dig. We take turns digging. We dig until we get down to the bottom. There is a river there, and a sun, and a moon that is made out of mud. See the moon, Girl tells us, her mouth ripping its grin across the face of it. It is a mirror. Look inside. Inside are two girls. Sisters. One for each brother. Girl points all of this out. Us brothers, we take a look inside. We see the two sisters, twins. We give each of us brothers a look, a shrug, then we dive inside. The moon shatters into a billion pieces. Each broken chunk becomes a star.

Star River

We go down to the river. We go down just before dark to watch for falling stars. The sky always darkens over the river first. Just after dark, Girl tells us brothers, this is the best time to catch a star that's falling. If Girl says this is so, then this is so. Look behind us, to the west of us, see the sky still holding onto its light. The star in the west, us brothers, we call that the sun. Girl calls it sister. Slowly the stars begin to take to the sky, each star is looking out a window curtained by day, shut to keep out its distant cousin, the sun. See that spoony-shaped thing there, Girl tells us brothers. We look to where Girl's pointy finger points. I call that Table. And that littler one over there, she says, that's its little brother. I call him Tea. I use Tea to stir up my morning cup of muddy river coffee. Table, Girl says, I use Table to sip from my bowl of muddy river soup for lunch. Us brothers, we don't doubt that any of this is true. If Girl says that this is so, then this is so. What about those stars way up there? Brother asks, looking straight up and above. Dust, Girl says. The sky is a house. Sometimes it gets dusty and dirty, muddy too. But the brother that I am sees something else to see. There! I cry out. Star, Girl! I point with my hand to where there is a smudge of fire smearing the sky. It is a burning matchstick, a still-lit cigarette flicked out the window of a speeding car. I try to picture the hand that threw this star. Try to imagine something bigger than Girl. I cannot. What I can see is this. I see Girl reach her right hand up into the sky. I see Girl catch this star from falling. See Girl take this star and hold it against her thigh, until it burns, until it leaves its mark.

Girl is a River

We watch Girl walk out into the river. She walks out into the river and she stops walking out when the river reaches up to her knees. Girl's knees are too lovely to be covered up. We call out stop at that exact moment that she herself stops her walking out. We say stop, and thank you, and wipe our hands across our brows. Girl stops and splashes some muddy water underneath her arms, over her head, her neck and breasts too. Her skin is a shining apple newly shucked of its skin. Us brothers must watch ourselves from wanting too much to take a bite out of Girl. Girl is a girl mud-naked, though it seems that this is a thing only us brothers can see.

A tugboat manned by a crew of ten men slugs on by, heading upriver, up through the legs of Girl, though they don't even toot a whistle or blow a horn. Hard hats laid off from the mill fish for catfish with the blood of lopped-off fingers, eyes locked on their stuck-in-the-mud fishing poles, tiny copper bells clipped to the poles' tips. Ring, ring, us brothers call this out. The fishermen grab hold of their fishing man poles. The men on board the tug turn towards the sound of our boy voices. Open your eyes, we holler. Look here, we point. See Girl, we say, because we want them to see what we see. Us brothers, we watch these men look around, up then down, into the muddy waters, up at the smokeless skies. These men see mud, they see mountain, they see smokestack and tree. River, we hear them whisper. Moon, they say. We tell them to look with their ears. We say to them the word, girl. Girl, we tell them. Say girl, we say. Say girl the way Girl was meant to be said: with twelve r's, thirteen u's and twenty thousand l's at the end of girl, rivering across the earth.

The Moon is a Lighthouse: Revisited

Our mother, underneath her breath, breathing so that us brothers can barely hear it, breathes, Bring me your river. We figure this, if only this, it is a thing us brothers can get ourselves to do. So we shove our mother's bed over to where the bedroom's window is a box of muddy light for our mother to look outside. Outside this window's pane, we can see it is raining. It's been raining so long now that we have run out of fingers for us to count the days on. This rain, it might never give up, we have given ourselves to believing. It might never stop. This is all right with us, for it's a good rain that makes for good mud making. And this, making mud, this is a thing us brothers can't never get enough of. But the moon. Brother, but the moon, it is another story. The moon is nowhere to be, by us brothers, seen. It is a brand new baseball lost in the bushes, or batted into some old man's backyard, broken through a neighbor's garage window. Or else it's a dog's bone buried in a backyard place we cannot get back to, the hole once dug now covered over and grown smooth with mud. See the river, we say, to our mother, and we sit her body up, our boy bodies two pillows stuck behind our mother's back. I can't see it, she says, her eye shades all a-flitter, the rainy light, dull as it is, to our mother's eyes, to moons used to only the dark: to her, this light is kisses, it is knives. The sky, we say to our mother next. Look at the sky. The sky, we say, it is a river. And the stars: the stars are the glowing eyes of fish. And the moon? our mother asks us brothers, catching us, her sons, off guard. The moon, we tell our mother, it is a lighthouse. And we are all of us living inside.

The Other Girl

Inside our father's shed there are hammers and nails and cigar boxes full of nuts and bolts and screws and a bottle half-filled with whiskey. This is what our father left us—this and his fishing poles with hooks still hooked on and his muddy steel-toed boots. There are these other things too: muddy buckets stuck inside muddy buckets, shovels muddy with rust, rolled up muddy hoses and ropes, a folded-up chair for sitting out on the lawn in, scrap pieces of saved-up, sawed-off lumber, a lantern-light to fish by at night, a net to scoop up the fish. Get the picture? And there's this other thing too: back behind the boxes of nuts and bolts and screws, back behind the bottles of whiskey, there is a twine-tied stack of magazines. Girls, I tell Brother, when he asks. There is this girl gazing out from the top of the pile. She is shirtless; she is shoving out her chest. I cannot tell you the color of her eyes. Holy moly! Brother says, his mud-colored eyes rolling open when he turns open the cover and begins flipping through. Look at that! What are those! Brother turns the magazine over onto its side and all of a sudden—all of a sudden!—this other girl comes, unfolding, fluttering, out. This girl, she is three pages long. She is wearing nothing on her body but a pair of red, spiky-heeled shoes. Believe me when I tell you, you have never seen teeth so white. Brother is a lighthouse light shining in the night. Get a load of those! Those are shoes, I tell him. No, not those! Those! Brother says, pointing them out. Headlights, I say. Brother says, They look more like balloons. I say the word, Moons. It is night. Us brothers, we read and we look by the light of our father's lantern. The glass glows with its inside fire. Our boy eyes are fallen stars still burning with all of these girls. After we are done doing this looking, we run ourselves down to the river. We each of us brothers pick up a stick by the edge of the muddy river's edge and stick it into the mud. At dawn, after a good night's sleep down by the river's muddy edge, we pull our sticks out from the mud. We take our stuck-in-the-mud sticks and write the word *girl* into the mud. G-I-R-L. Girl. The muddy river washes in, in waves, to cover up with muddy water the word girl. Us brothers, with Girl in between us, we drop down onto our hands and knees, down in the mud, and begin to eat.

Nails

Girl said moon, though she wasn't looking up at the sky. What she was looking at was our hands, at our muddy boy fingers, pointing down at the half-moons of light shining underneath the nails. Our nails, they were gnawed-to-the-nubs, mud-caked, muddy-stained stubs. Our hands, fingers, they were the fingers and hands of boys. Our boy knuckles were rivers. Our palms, held up to the sky, could hold up whole mountains. And they did. Take a look at Girl's. We made Girl's with our own two hands. Girl's peaks are twin, mud-topped wonders that inspire the break-up of clouds. We make clouds, down here below, when we wash our muddy hands in the river. The moon's light shines down above the head of Girl; it shines until Girl, she is a just shadow of mud and smoke that holds the river in its place. Don't go, says the moon. Us brothers, we listen to moon. We sink ourselves down, into the mud, and hold our hands up to the light, up to the moon that slips its slippered foot in beneath our finger's muddy nails—this moon that we nibble on, that we gnaw our way towards. To get down to the half-light. To that shining underneath.

The Singing Fish

One night Girl takes us brothers by the mud of our hands, down to the river, and in a circle, and under the moon's light, and with fish nibbling on our ankles and toes, the fish's silver fins knifing through these muddy waters, like this, us brothers, we begin to sing. We sing with Girl, with Girl twirling us brothers around, spinning us round and round on this Ferris wheel of river and rust and mud, until us brothers singing takes us up to a place high inside the sky, up where we can see that the stars are actually fires. Campfires, bonfires, fires stoked and kept burning by the windmilled breath of Girl. Us brothers, we are brothers fascinated by fire. This fuzzy white light of star-fire is hard for our eyes to look at, but still we look at it, we gaze straight into it, our fingers reach out towards it, to touch this fire, because we want to know how fire feels—how it feels to burn. Us brothers, we can't resist it. We stick our hands, unfisted, into this fire. We feel around, inside fire, until we find fire's star-shaped heart. This heart, it is sharp to our fingers' touches. It is five-armed and fifty-fingered. We pull its hands. We pull and we pull and we keep on pulling, until our hands explode in our face.

Good, Brothers

We come home one day after being gone all day long fishing for fish in the river only to find standing inside of our house people other than us. There is a mother other than our mother, there is a father other than our father, there are two boys in our house who are brothers other than us. Our mother and our father turn their faces to face the sounds us brothers are making when we come boots bursting into our house, in through the back door, and what they say, our mother and our father, not to us but to this other family other than us is, these are our two boys. Who are they? is what us brothers say to what we see standing inside our house. This other family, this other mother and this other father and these two brothers other than us, they look almost too much like us to be us; it could be us looking into some sort of a mirror. But they are not us, and we are not them, and what our father says to us, to our question, who are they? is, he says to us, his sons, that this is the family that might be moving into this house. This is our house, Brother points this out. There's not room enough for all of us inside of this house. That's true, our mother says to this, and for the first time in a long time, she is actually smiling. Which is why, our mother tells us, if Mr. and Mrs. Ditoro decide that they want to buy our house from us, then we'll have to find some other house for us to live in. We like this house, us brothers say to this. Let them find some other house to live in. Maybe this is a bad time, the other mother says to our mother. The other father says to our father that maybe it would be better if they came back another time. Our mother shakes her head. Our father nods his and says yes, he'll call them later. When our father says this, our mother shoots our father this look across the space that is between them. It's a look that could, with just one look, turn a muddy river into dirt and ice. Boys, our mother says to us, looking this look down to us, what do you say you take the Ditoro boys outside to look at your fish. Us brothers stand across from and we stare into the eyes of these boys who are brothers not to us. All four of us boys, us staring across our house at each other, to our mother saying that word *fish*, we each of us nod with our boy heads yes. That sounds good to us, us brothers say. Outside, we go with these other brothers out back to the back of our backyard, to show these boys what our mother meant to say when she said that word fish. Fish? What kind of fish? is what these other brothers ask us. Our fish, is what we tell them, and we lift our hands up to get these boys to see our backyard telephone pole that is studded and shining with the hammered-in heads of fish. We had us a river once, one of these boys says to this, his head still tilted up. Our river, it was a real good river for catching fish. Our river is the muddiest river ever made, is what us brothers tell these boys. So what are you brothers gonna do? is the thing that these other brothers want to be told. How, we hear these brothers saying to us, are you gonna get them to let you stay? Us brothers, we look at these brothers. We look at these brothers the way that us brothers look at our fish. After a while, when we are done looking at these other brothers like this, us brothers, we give each other this same sort of a look. Brother is the brother of us brothers who walks away from this look. Brother is going, only I know, to get what we need to get us to stay. I am the one of us brothers who stays right where I am standing. I am facing into the faces of these other brothers. Then I tell these other brothers to stand right here, not to go away, to wait, stay, I say, stand right here, I tell them, with your backs backed up against our fish-headed pole. Facing the river. We'll show you the river, I say, to myself, just as soon as us brothers get back. And then I walk, I go, out back to where Brother is behind us all standing, with a rusty-clawed hammer dangling from each one of his fists. I give Brother this look. We both know what this look means. We are brothers. We are each other's voice inside our own heads. Brother holds out the hammer. I reach out for Brother's hand. Good, Brother, I say. When we get back to those other brothers, they are right where we left them, right where we told them to stay standing behind, with their backs and their boot-heels backed up against our fish-headed pole. Good, brothers, us brothers say to these boys. Now give us your hands, we tell them. To this, these other brothers, they do what we say. We are brothers, after all; these boys are more than just boys. Now this might sting, we tell them, and we take each of these brothers each by his hand and we hold them up to the pole's creosoted wood. Both of these brothers, they take the nail to their hands—yes, just like brothers. They don't wince, or flinch with their bodies, or make with their boy mouths the sounds of a brother crying out. Good, brothers, we say these words again. We are both of us brothers both of us getting ready to hammer a second nail into these other brothers' other hands when our mothers and our fathers, all four of them, step out into the back of our backyard. Sons, our fathers call us out. All four of us boys, all of us brothers, we turn back our heads toward the sound of our fathers. It's time to come home, we hear our mothers say. Us brothers, we turn back to face each other. Our faces are facing back with each other. Up above us, in this sky above the river, in this sky above the mill, the moon, it is just now beginning to rise. In the light of this light, us brothers, we raise back our hammers. We line up those rusted nails.

The Moon is a Lighthouse: Revisited

Girl is down by the river, Girl, she is down on her hands and knees, and what Girl is doing is, she is building a tower made out of slags of rusted steel. For us brothers to climb is what Girl tells us when we ask her why, and what for, and what is she doing? So we can look her eye to eye, Girl adds. It is three days later now and what we are doing is, we are climbing this made-out-of-slag tower that Girl has up-from-the-river's-mud built, our boy hands gloved with the mud of us brothers bleeding. But us brothers—we don't care about us bleeding. Below us, the steel mill, it is barely a square, it is a matchbox dropped down upon this muddy earth. And the mud-rusty river that runs its way through this dirty river town: it is just a wrinkle in the palm of a held-open hand. Here, up at the top, what us brothers see, when we get a close-up look into Girl's eyes, when we see them the way they were meant to be seen—see them the way they were made to be looked inside of: we see moons floating in a river of muddy water. Each moon is a lighthouse with us brothers living inside.

Mud Love

Not everybody loved mud the way that us brothers loved mud. Us brothers, we learned this the hard way. We learned this the same way we learned that not everybody in the world believed that Girl was more than just, to us brothers, some made-out-of-mud dream.

Blindness, Brother said.

Brother, we shook our boy heads, they just don't see.

They threw rocks and bricks. They took axes to Girl as if Girl was a tree. They knocked Girl down. They chopped Girl into pieces. They left Girl down at the muddy river's edge—to die, to wash back into muddy water, to turn back into mud.

They made us watch but we couldn't watch. We closed our eyes even though they told us we couldn't. We rolled our eyeballs back into the backs of our sockets, back inside that place where what you see is mostly made up of mud and water and light.

We built Girl back up, from the ground up, from the bottom, beginning at her girl feet, the very next night, when nobody was watching. She began again as mud. We made her into Girl. When we were done making Girl out of mud, Girl said that she didn't remember anything of what had happened. She said this like she was just waking up out of a bad dream that she knew she'd had but she could not say what the dream was about. We didn't know where to begin. So we told Girl the truth—about rocks and bricks. Then we told a lie. We said they thought she was a tree. So make me into a mountain, she said.

So we did.

We made her twice as big.

We watched as Girl took two stars and stuck them in her eyes.

Girl ate the moon.

She blew out the sun's fire.

She dunked her hands into the river.

Girl drank until there was nothing left but mud.

Girl: Revisited

We walked through that place where town used to be, where now there was just a river muddily flowing. We were the three of us, here at the dead end of the road, two brothers with Girl in between us, our hands hooked in that crook of where Girl's elbow made the shape of a sideways laying V. Here, where town used to be, there was just the river and a handful of shipwrecked buildings watching over where the muddy waters continued to still flow—so many doors waiting to be opened, windows without people to look through them, each rust-colored brick trapped by the weight of what held it in its place. Town was the place we used to go to with our mother or father when our mother or father needed some little something to get from the town hardware store where our father used to talk nuts and bolts and fixing things with old man Higgerson with the one leg that was lost in the war, who stood there and listened and nodded his head and sometimes, after our father was done saying what he had to say, Mister Higgerson liked to tell us brothers how it was that he lost the leg that was missing from where it used to be right there on his body. What I remember most about what he liked to tell us was that the next thing Mister Higgerson knew, he was waking up in some place his eyes had never before seen, and when he reached down to scratch at the place where his right leg used to be, there was no leg there for him to scratch, even though, he liked us brothers to know this, it still itched him there like there was still a leg there for him to scratch. Us brothers, we told Girl this story, about this one leg that was missing, and what Girl wanted to know was, what happened to the leg after it was gone? This was a thing that us brothers, we did not know this, about the leg, and now it is too late to ask, because not only is Mister

Higgerson's leg gone, but now Mister Higgerson himself is gone away from this dirty river place, though the nuts and bolts that he used to sell are still sitting there inside, rusting inside cardboard boxes that are still sitting on the dust-rusty shelves. But what happened after? This is the question that Girl cannot get her mind past. We tell her we don't know. We tell her about our father, about him walking out, into the river, that muddy kind of sky, leaving us brothers with just the sound that a river sometimes makes when a stone is skipped across it. He was gone, but a part of him was and is still here, just like the itch that old Mister Higgerson always felt in that space where his leg used to be. Us brothers, we tell Girl, we went out looking for our father, but what we found was better than father. Girl looks at us brothers and wants to know what could be better than father? Do we have to spell it out? we say. We give Girl this look. There is this look that us brothers, we sometimes like to look at each other with this look. It is the kind of a look that actually hurts the face of the brother who is doing the looking. Imagine that look. This is the look that we look at Girl with. Give me a stick, Brother says. He takes hold of a branch from a nearby tree and Brother breaks it off. He takes this stick and uses it as a pencil, and the earth is a piece of paper that he is moving his hand across. Brother writes what it was that we found, what word it was that was better than us finding our father, and the word is girl. But the word, girl, the way that Girl was meant to be spelled: with twelve r's, thirteen u's, and twenty thousand l's at the end of girl, stretching across the earth.

Where the Fire Is

This is what we want you to see: see the two of us brothers out on our dirty river, this river rusty with mud, us brothers on a rusty-bottomed rowboat that is a boat made out of steel. This boat, it is a boat that our father once told us brothers, it wasn't fit to float sardines. Us brothers, we are not minnowy little fish. We are big muddy boys. We are muddy brothers out on a rusty rowboat that is drifting sideways down a mud-rusty river: two brothers floating between these two in-between-us worlds. It's the mud of the river that is holding us brothers up. For all us brothers know, for all we care, this river, it could be the sky. No, this is not some kind of a dream. No, when the two of us brothers dream, we dream of mud and moon and fish and Girl. Girl, she is right now somewhere where our eyes cannot see. But over there, wherever Girl is, the sun, it is sure to be shining. The sun, right now, it is not shining here on us. Over our heads, in this sky that is a river all bottom-stirry with mud and clouds, zigzags of light, axes of lightning, chainsaws of it, busted bicycle chains of it, razor down from the sky to set oak trees and leaning-over pole barns on fire—white jags of light slashing down to set on fire all of those things made out of steel: golf clubs and baseball bats, town water towers and smokestacks, electrical poles, boats up on land, boats out on river's water. Our boat, with the two of us brothers in it, we are out on the water. Yes, we are out on water but we are surrounded by, we are brothers about to be swallowed by, sky. This sky above us, the whole river of it, where only moments ago we could still see blue, it is now nothing but, it is now every bit of it, mud. When we look up, us brothers, we could be looking up from beneath the ground—two earthworms testing the mud to see if it is raining. When the rains start to hammer on down upon us brothers, buckets of it, barrels of it, whole big ore boats of it raining down, our boat, which had up until now been filled up to the gunnels of it with fish—the fishes' silver fish bodies glinting the color of newly-made metal—our boat, it is filling up, it is fastly flowing over first from rain water and then with river water and then we, us brothers, and our boat, like this, we begin to sink. The fish in our boat float out and away from us brothers, back down the river—a basket of fish-birds released back into the sky. Us brothers, we are up to our ankles, we are up to our knees, we are up to the necks of us brothers, when we wave goodbye to these getting-away fish. Then us brothers, we get it into our boy heads for us to run. We run on top of water, through both rain and river, across the water, us brothers, we run. See us running brothers run: running to reach the river's muddy shore: us brothers running to outrun the rivers of light chain-sawing down, veins of it, spikes of it spiking the earth, the dirt, the river, the steel: bent-back nails of hammering light seeking us brothers out, us brothers who cry out to the sky above us, come and try to get us! This, we dare the sky this, we dare to dare this, with our boy fists raised up to whatever is up there listening. This is us brothers running towards those places where the light has lit up all that is dark: us brothers running to see which brother of us will get there first—running until us brothers run ourselves out of breath: running until the light gets its bead and its hammer's head of lightning over both of our boy heads. Boy, are we starting to feel it now: see how the hair on our heads stands up at a bristle so that it is looking to get itself a closer look. Us brothers, we stop and we turn so that our eyes might get a good look at it, too—the way the sky swings its hammer right above our boy heads. We stop and we turn and we reach out with our hands. Us brothers, the both of us know, this won't hurt a bit. We hold out our hands and the rivers there, our knuckles, our palms, they are all filled with singing fish. We open our eyes wide and we listen to this song. It is a song that says, let me hold your hand. Us brothers, we look around looking for Girl. We see a cloud in the sky that is the shape of a hand. No, it *is* a hand. It's a hand that us brothers, we watch it reach down to take hold of us brothers both of us by the wrists. We do not try to do anything to wrestle our hands free from this. Us brothers, we hold our hands wide open, with our fingers flared out and wriggling, the backs of our hands backing up all the way up, back against the backdrop of sky. Our hands backed up against the sky makes a sound that knuckles sometimes make when they knock up against wood. What sound we hear next is not the sound of thunder or of rainwater running down a steel roof. It is the sound of a voice saying, coming. Us brothers, we turn back around to face where this sound is coming from. What we see, when we turn back to see this coming sound, is half of the sky—it is opening up: it is a door. Who is it? we hear us brothers being asked. Us, is all us brothers have to say. It is Girl's voice, we can tell, who is the one doing the asking, and Girl's hand is the hand that is opening this door up. Come in, Girl tells us. Get out of the rain. You're sopping wet. We do what Girl tells us. We come in out of the rain. Inside, there is a fire burning in the fireplace: there is hot soup simmering on the stove. Our mother, she is sweeping the wood floors, not with a broom but with a sunflower. She looks over at us and yes, our mother, at us brothers, her face unfolds its smile. She looks almost beautiful now, almost happy, with the sun, the sunflower, held like this in her brooming hands. We come inside, brother followed by brother, rain water and river water rivering down from our heads. Our boots, wet and muddy, we take them off, we set them by the door. It's good to be back home, we say this to our mother. Us brothers, we look at each other with our look. We keep on looking with this look. Then we run over to where the fire is burning and we throw us brothers in.

The River at the End of the River

We see mud, we see dirt where the river is, we see this earth that us brothers once walked across. Brother wants to know, Where's it going? So I say to him, Let's go see. We keep our eyes on the flowing mud, the drifting dirt. We walk alongside of the river until the river comes to its end. Water is nowhere. Mud everywhere. Here there is dirt. Here the earth is flat. Let's keep going, I say. I take Brother's hand. We walk, hand in hand, towards the edge of this brother world. Behind us, where the new day's sun lifts its lips to kiss the sky red, a hundred thousand girls, other than Girl, naked beneath their mud skins, they rise up out of the mud. These other girls, they are a mountain of mud. These girls, they strip the sun of its sky. Us brothers, we walk out into the muddy dark. Night is leading us brothers blind. We walk and we walk until there is nothing left to hold us brothers up, until mud and dirt drops out from under our mud-covered boots. Brothers, we are falling. No, we are brothers floating. We are brothers rising up. The moon, it is a white-ringed buoy tossed to us brothers by the hand that is the hand of Girl. Us brothers, we take turns kicking our legs, flapping our wings, lifting up with our heads. Until we begin to fly.

Mud Soup

One night we see, down by the river, we see Girl. Girl is down by the river, down on her hands and knees, down in the river-made mud, and Girl is doing with mud what us brothers, we do not know what it is she is doing. I am making a pot, is what she tells us, when us brothers ask her what is she doing. When we ask Girl why after Girl tells us brothers about making a pot, that she is making it out of mud, Girl looks at us brothers with this hungry kind of a look looking out from her girl eyes, and then Girl tells us that she is making a pot for her to make soup in. Soup, we say this to ourselves. What kind of soup? is what is next on our list of what we want from Girl to know. Climb in and take a look, is what Girl says to this. Us brothers, we do what Girl says. We climb up this pot's muddy sides and we dive down inside. Inside of this made-out-of-mud pot there is muddy river water filled up to the pot's top. This water is good and muddy, just the way us brothers like it. There are some rusted jags of slag metal jutting up from the bottom of the pot, while up on top, floating on the water's muddy skin, are the chopped-off heads and moon-shining eyes of dead fish gazing up. When we point all of this out to Girl, what Girl says to us is that this, the rusted metal, the fish heads, the fish eyes, this is all for the soup's flavor. Without this, Girl tells us brothers, this soup would be nothing but muddy water. I almost forgot, she then says, I need wood for the fire. Girl turns then and we watch her walk up away from the river, heading towards the woods that come between the river and the shipwrecked-in-the-mud mill. When Girl comes back, she is holding in her girl arms an armful of ten-foot-tall trees, the dirt and the dirty roots still dangling from that part of the tree that was born closest to the earth. Us brothers, we poke our boy heads up over the rim of this mud pot to see Girl slide these trees up underneath this pot's muddy bottom and then we watch her set them on fire. Girl takes two of these trees and rubs them together to start a fire. It doesn't take long for the water to heat up. Bath time, Girl says, when the bubbles start up boiling. Girl sticks a muddy finger into the bubbling water and tells us brothers that we're just about ready. When the skin of us brothers begins to pull away from the bone, it only hurts us just a little. It only hurts us just a little the way sometimes it used to hurt just a little bit too when our mother used to hold our mud-covered hands under hot running water to get the caked mud to come washing off. When the skin slides off of the bone, and the muscles beneath the skin are tender and red, this is when Girl knows we are ready. She spoons us up, one brother per hand, and begins to eat.

Good, Brother: Revisited

Girl says to us brothers, You were born with the same hands. She takes hold of our dirty boy palms and unfolds them open into maps. Take a look, Girl says. See that star in the middle? Look closer and you'll see it's an eye. Brother wants to know, whose eye is it? It's the eye, Girl says, you use to see when it's dark. Close your eyes, Girl tells us brothers. Then you'll see what I mean. Us brothers, we close our eyes just like Girl tells us. Good, Girl whispers. Now hold out your hands in front of your face, your palms facing away. Tell me what you see. We see river, I say. We see fish. We see moon. Mud, I say. I see Girl. Good, Girl says, to this. Now, open your eyes back up. Look into the palm of your right hand. We look. The star that was in our hand, in its middle, it is now an eye. It is an eyeball as big as a baseball is. It is lid-less, is blink-less, its pupil, it is a wide open sky that is the color of mud. There is this river there, running through it, and a moon floating whitely above. Inside, I can see the face of Girl gazing up at us brothers. But Brother is the brother of us who sees with a different kind of an eye. The eye in his hand sees words different. Where I see river, fish, moon, Brother says rust, hammer, nail. When I ask him why this is so, when I say, Why, Brother, why? Brother holds open his right hand. There is an eyeball right here, in Brother's hand, too, but the white of this eye is mud-shot, it is bloody with mud and the rust of a rusted, bent-back nail. If I had a hammer, Brother says. This, the sound of this, it is a threat. He raises up his hammering hand, says again, If I only had a hammer. I see Girl reach down then, into the river, and pull out from its riverness, from beneath its mudness, a hammer dripping with mud. I watch as Girl hands this fished-up-from-the-river hammer into Brother's hammering hand. There is this hammer and then Girl also gives to Brother a handful of un-hammered nails. Now it's your turn, Brother tells me. It's true: I knew the time would come. And so I take it just like a brother. I take three steps back until I'm standing beneath the bridge that is Girl's legs. Girl's legs, they are tree trunks that reach up toward the sky and meet half the way there to form an upside down letter V. I take hold of Girl by the backs of her made-out-of-mud knees. The skin back here, hidden away, it is skin newborn, it is delicate, it is almost too soft for a brother to touch. I said, almost. And so I touch it. The current of the river is running through my hand. I start to pull back, to pull it away, but I can't. Brother has me by the hand. He has a hammer in his other. The handful of half a dozen nails sticking out from his mouth could be a mouthful of teeth. Brother is a brother who is grinning now. It is the grin of a brother who is giving back to his brother a taste of his own river. This boy I call Brother—he is the bigger of us brothers right now. I can't help but close my eyes. But the eye in my hand, it still sees it all. The eye in the middle of my hand, it sees the swing of the hammer going back; it sees the lining up of this nail. Then the eye in my hand opens up wide, it opens up wider than the sky. Sees a light and lightning burning through. Good, Brother. This is the sound that my ears hear. Then the voice of Girl booming out, telling us brothers, it's time for us, for all of this, to stop. This voice, only this voice, us brothers listen to this. Brother takes me by my hand and Brother takes my hand and he washes it in the river. The eye in my hand, it is a fish out of water. It is a fish waiting to be set free. Girl whispers into my ear for me to close my hand, to squeeze it tight, as tight as I can, as if I am holding onto something that I could not live without. What I picture is Girl. Girl is in the palm of my hand. I squeeze my hand that tight. Good, Girl says. Now open up your hand. I do what she says. I unfold my fingers, little by little. I open my eyes. There is this bird, there, it is a pigeon, sitting in my hand. Hey, I say. A bird. It's a cloud, Girl tells me. Then Girl tells this thing in my hand to fly and fly away. This bird, it lifts itself up into the sky. See it fly and climb above the head that is Girl's as it heads downriver, downwind, growing bigger and bigger the further it moves away, flying and flying and flapping its wings until the tips of its feathers stretch from one end of the sky all the way to the other, a great big bird of a cloud that our father liked to tell us brothers, Boys, in the end, this is where the river is.

But us brothers, we did not believe this to be true.

Us brothers, we knew better.

Us brothers knew that the river was a place here on this earth.

Us brothers knew that what our father said when he said this cloud is where the river is was, in truth, a bird. It was a bird that was once a fish that was once an eye that was once, back in the beginning, it was a star in the middle of our boy hands.